KU-300-820

Witches

Iris Howden

NEWCASTLE-UNDER-LYME
COLLEGE LIBRARY

Published in association with
The Basic Skills Agency

Newcastle Under Lyme College

DC022420

Acknowledgements
Cover: Matthew Williams
Illustrations: Jim Eldridge

Orders; please contact Bookpoint Ltd, 39 Milton Park, Abingdon, Oxon OX14
4TD. Telephone: (44) 01235 400414, Fax: (44) 01235 400454. Lines are open
from 9.00–6.00, Monday to Saturday, with a 24 hour message answering service.
Email address: orders@bookpoint.co.uk

British Library Cataloguing in Publication Data
A catalogue record for this title is available from the British Library

ISBN 0 340 77606 4

First published 2000
Impression number 10 9 8 7 6 5 4 3 2 1
Year   2005 2004 2003 2002 2001 2000

Copyright © 2000 Iris Howden

All rights reserved. No part of this publication may be reproduced or transmitted
in any form or by any means, electronic or mechanical, including photocopying,
recording or any information storage and retrieval system, without permission in
writing from the publisher or under licence from the Copyright Licensing Agency
Limited. Further details of such licences (for reprographic reproduction) may be
obtained from the Copyright Licensing Agency Limited, of 90 Tottenham Court
Road, London W1P 9HE.

Typeset by GreenGate Publishing Services, Tonbridge, Kent.
Printed in Great Britain for Hodder and Stoughton Educational, a division of
Hodder Headline Plc, 338 Euston Road, London NW1 3BH, by Atheneum
Press, Gateshead, Tyne & Wear

Witches

Contents

FIC HOW
NEWCASTLE-UNDER-LYME
COLLEGE LIBRARY
DC022420

1

The Cottage

It was stuffy in the car.
Alison had cramp in her legs.
She tried to move them
but a box of food was in the way.
'There's no room in this car,' she moaned.
'Move your rucksack over a bit, Jamie.'
'Never mind,' Mum said. 'We're nearly there.'
She looked at the map again.
'Take the next on the left,' she told Dad.

Outside, rain fell non-stop.
The hills were hidden by the mist.
'So much for the famous Pendle Hill,'
Alison said.
'You can't even see it in this weather.
Think of Kate and Lisa lying on the beach.'
'Don't start on that again,' Mum said.
You're too young to go on holiday alone.'
She sounded cross so Alison kept quiet.

She was still put out. Her best friends
were off having a good time in Spain.
She was stuck with a family holiday.
A holiday in Lancashire of all places.
In a cottage, with only her Mum and Dad
and her young brother for company.
Life was a real pain sometimes.

So was Jamie's Walkman.
The ching ching ching of his tapes playing
got on her nerves.
She poked him in the ribs.
Jamie took his headphones off.

on thought.
Dad as well.
' overtime.'
ut the way she'd acted
e.
ke it up with Jamie.
're reading?' she asked.
ut the witches of Pendle,'
und it in my bedroom.
 says here:

families of witches lived

two old women called
attox."

daughter was called Alizon
amie said.
is spelled with a z not an s.
e initials as you, AD.
Alison Davies.

'What's up now Ali?' he asked.
'Turn that thing off for a bit,' Alison said.
'It's driving me mad. And don't call me Ali.'

'Will you two please stop it,' Dad said.
He drew up in front of a grey stone cottage.
'We're here. Help me unload the car you two.'
Jamie ran inside with his rucksack.
Alison was left to carry in the box of food.
It was very heavy.
'Trust Jamie to skive off,' she thought.
By the time she got inside Jamie
had been up and bagged the best room.
She was left with a small one at the back.

It looked out onto the churchyard.
The graves were a mass of weeds.
It looked quite spooky in the mist.
Alison went across the room
to hang her clothes in the wardrobe.
The floor creaked under her feet.
'Great,' she said. 'That's all I need.
A holiday in a haunted house.'

'What's up now Ali?' he asked.
'Turn that thing off for a bit,' Alison said.
'It's driving me mad. And don't call me Ali.'

'Will you two please stop it,' Dad said.
He drew up in front of a grey stone cottage.
'We're here. Help me unload the car you two.'
Jamie ran inside with his rucksack.
Alison was left to carry in the box of food.
It was very heavy.
'Trust Jamie to skive off,' she thought.
By the time she got inside Jamie
had been up and bagged the best room.
She was left with a small one at the back.

It looked out onto the churchyard.
The graves were a mass of weeds.
It looked quite spooky in the mist.
Alison went across the room
to hang her clothes in the wardrobe.
The floor creaked under her feet.
'Great,' she said. 'That's all I need.
A holiday in a haunted house.'

Downstairs Jamie was trying to get a picture
on the TV. It was a very old set.
'This thing's out of the dark ages,' he said.
'Look at it. The picture's all fuzzy.'
'Turn it off,' Mum said.
'You'll hurt your eyes.
You watch too much TV anyway.'
She went into the kitchen
and began to bang pots and pans about.
This was a bad sign.
The family kept out of her way
when she did this.

'Your Mum's tired,' Dad said.
'Let's all try to help her this week.
She works hard. She needs a rest.
It means a lot to her to come up here.
She's very keen to trace her family tree.
You two are old enough to go off
and do your own thing.
If we're better off next year,
we'll do something more exciting.
Maybe go abroad, OK?'

'He's right,' Alison thought.
'Mum is tired, Dad as well.
He does a lot of overtime.'
She felt bad about the way she'd acted
on the way there.
She tried to make it up with Jamie.
'What's that you're reading?' she asked.
'It's a book about the witches of Pendle,'
Jamie said. 'I found it in my bedroom.
Listen to this. It says here:

*"In the 1600s two families of witches lived
near Pendle Hill.
They were led by two old women called
Demdike and Chattox."*

'Demdike's grandaughter was called Alizon
– just like you,' Jamie said.
'Only her name is spelled with a z not an s.
She had the same initials as you, AD.
Alizon Device – Alison Davies.

'Just think she might have lived
in this cottage.
What if you're Alizon Device
come to life again?
The same person living again
for a second time.'

'Don't be so stupid,' Alison said.
'That's rubbish!'
Jamie loved to scare her.
He spent his life telling her horror stories.
She tried to take no notice.
But she often felt afraid all the same.
She didn't look forward to going to bed.
This dark cottage was miles from anywhere.
Outside the wind was howling.
It sounded like someone crying.
She grabbed Jamie's Walkman.
She clamped it on her head
and tried to drown out the noise of the wind.

2

The Egg Man

The next day was sunny and warm.
'I'll make a start at the record office,'
Mum said.
'I've got a list of names to follow up.'
'I'll drive you in,' Dad said.
'Do you two want to come to town?'
'I'd rather stay here,' Jamie said.
'Suss out the village.'
'Me too,' Alison said. 'We'll be OK.'
'There's plenty of food in the fridge,'
Mum said. 'We'll be back by tea time.'

Alison walked up the village street.
It looked pretty in the sunshine.
The old cottages stood in neat rows.
Their gardens were bright with flowers.
The Post Office was the only shop.
There was a pub, a church
and a village green. That was all.
Then she saw a phone box.
'I'll give Kelly a ring,' she thought.
'See if she's heard from Kate and Lisa.'
The four girls went around together at school.
Alison looked in her purse.
All she had was a five pound note.

An old man was pushing a hand-cart
down the street.
He was knocking on doors selling eggs.
'I'll ask him if he's got change,'
Alison thought.
She went up to him. He looked a bit odd.
He was small and fat with thick glasses.
He wore a straw hat on his head.

'Excuse me,' Alison said.
'Have you any change?
I want to make a phone call.'
'No I haven't,' the man said in a rude way.
'Well, thanks for nothing,' Alison thought.
Nasty old so and so. He never even looked.
'I hope the wheels fall off your cart,'
she said softly to herself.

She walked on. A big black dog
came out of a garden.
It ran up to her and stopped.
Alison patted it on the head.
'What do you want, boy?' she asked.
The dog barked – as if it was trying
to answer her. Alison laughed.
'Good boy, go home,' she said.
The dog trotted off, just as if
it had understood.

Suddenly at the end of the street
she saw the old man fall down.
He lay in the road on his back.

His eggs slid from the cart.
They fell to the ground and broke.
Alison ran to help him.
He pushed her out of the way.
He limped away, pushing his cart.
Alison felt terrible.
She did not really wish him any harm.

She went back to the cottage.
Jamie was sitting at the table eating.

'That's a mega plate of sandwiches,'
Alison said. 'Have you left any food for me?'
Jamie looked up from his book.
'What's a pedlar?' he asked.
'A man who used to go round door to door,'
Alison told him. 'Selling ribbons,
pins and stuff.
Why do you want to know?'
Jamie began to read aloud. 'It says here:

"Alison Device is begging on the road to Colne.
A pedlar refuses her some pins
and she curses him.
Suddenly a black dog appears and she orders
it to lame the pedlar.
He collapses and is paralysed on the left side."

Alison went cold all over.
She grabbed the book from Jamie's hand.
She wanted to read the words for herself.
She went over in her mind
what had happened that morning.

The old man had been selling
eggs door to door.
The black dog had come from nowhere.
It had seemed to speak to her.
The words she had used to the egg man
were a sort of curse.
She thought about Jamie joking last night.
'What if you're Alizon Device
come to life again.'

'Hey, I was reading that,' Jamie said.
'What's the matter, Ali?
You look as white as a sheet.'
'Shush a minute,' Alison said.
She began to skim through the book.

It said that Alizon Device had been taken
before the Squire.
He made her confess that she was a witch.
Alizon said her grandmother had made her
become one. She told the Squire
that the Chattox family were also witches.

They had put spells on people.
They had made clay figures
and stuck pins in them.

Alison read on.
The two families were sent
to Lancaster Castle.
They were kept in jail there.
At their trial, Jennet, Alizon's
nine-year-old sister, stood up on a table.
She spoke out against them.
She pointed the finger at her own family.
They were all found guilty and hanged.

Alison handed the book back to Jamie.
Her hand was shaking.
She did not say anything to him.
He would only make things worse
by teasing her.
Besides, what could she tell him?
He would think she was crazy if she said
she had lamed a man – just like Alizon Device.
But she felt afraid. She wished they had
never come to this horrible place.

3

Lancaster Castle

'We're going to Lancaster today,' Mum said
at breakfast the next day. 'Want to come?'
'Yes please,' Alison said quickly.
Anything to get away from the village.
'What is there in Lancaster?' Jamie asked.
'There's quite a lot to see,' Dad told him.
'It's an old town, by the River Lune.
There are a couple of museums, a castle,
lots of shops.'
'OK,' Jamie said.
'But I'll pass on the museums.'

It was a lovely drive through the hills.
The sun was shining and Alison felt better.
She began to look forward to their day out.
When they got there they split up.
Dad took Jamie to look at the river.
Alison and her Mum
looked around the shops.
They had agreed to meet at a café later.

When they got there it was crowded.
There was no sign of Dad and Jamie.
'Get a table,' Mum said.
'I'll join the queue.'
Alison sat at a table near the window.

There was something on the chair next to her.
She picked it up,
then dropped it again quickly.
It was a little figure shaped like a man.
It had a badge
with a pin stuck through its body.

It gave Alison a shock.
She stared at it in horror.
The book said the witches
had made clay figures.
Here was one right in front of her.
She grabbed the little figure.
It was made of playdough.
Quickly, Alison pulled out the pin.
She rolled the playdough into a ball.
Then she smashed it flat with her fist.

'Mummy, Mummy she's spoiled my little man!'
A child was standing next to her, shouting.
She was pointing a finger at Alison.
Alison looked up to see a woman
and a small girl staring at her.
Feeling very silly, she handed over
the ball of playdough.
She gave the badge to the child.
Dad and Jamie came in at that moment.
Alison tried to forget what had happened.

After lunch Mum went off to a church.
She wanted to check some names
in the parish register.
The others went to visit the castle.
Alison didn't really want to go
but she didn't fancy being on her own.
'Besides,' she thought, 'I might as well see
the place where the witches' story ended.
The place where they all died.'

The castle was built of grey stone.
It looked a grim place.
Alison imagined how the witches
must have felt when they were brought there.
A guide showed them around.
He asked them all to step into a cell.
Then he shut the heavy door with a slam.
It was pitch dark inside. Alison felt scared.
In her mind she could hear the cries
of the prisoners in the past.
She felt as if she could not breathe.
She was glad when the door opened again.

Mum was pleased with her day's work.
Back at the cottage she spread papers
over the table.
'I'd like to leave these out and work
on them in the morning,' she said.
'Let's go over to the pub. I'll treat us all
to a bar meal tonight.'

The pub was a real country pub.
It had horse brasses on the walls.
A log fire laid in the grate.
A boy with dark hair took their order.
His name was Nick.
He was really nice and friendly.
He asked Mum and Dad about their holiday.
He joked with Jamie about his football team.
His smile made Alison feel special.

It was a good evening –
until Jamie spoiled it.
Back at the cottage he said to Alison,
'Mind you don't cast a spell on Nick.'
'What are you talking about?' Alison said.
'Well, it says in that book that the witches
killed the son of the landlord at the inn.
They made a clay image of him.
They stuck pins in it and he died.'

'Will you stop going on about witches,'
Alison shouted. 'I'm sick of your silly games.
It's all nonsense. I'm going to bed.'

Alison didn't sleep well that night.
She had a bad dream. She dreamt
she was on trial in Lancaster Castle.
Lots of people sat watching her.
The child from the café was there.
She stood up on a table.
She pointed a finger at Alison.
'She did it,' the little girl shouted.
'The witch killed the landlord's son.
I saw her make a clay figure of him.
I heard her say the magic spell.
She did it. She did it. She did it.'

Alison woke up in a sweat.
The room was pitch black.
For a moment she thought she really was
in a cell in Lancaster Castle.
She switched on the light
and looked at her watch.
It was four o'clock in the morning.
She didn't get back to sleep again that night.

4

Pendle Hill

'Admit it,' Alison said to Jamie. 'We're lost.
I should never have trusted you with the map.
Give it to me.' She was cross and tired
after a night with hardly any sleep.
Her legs ached from the climb up Pendle Hill.
Why had she let Jamie talk her into this hike?

The day had started out sunny and bright.
Now, black rain clouds filled the sky.
A heavy mist hid the valley below.
They walked for ages looking for the path.

The grass there was the tough moorland kind.
There were boggy patches everywhere.
Alison's feet were soon wet.
Her new trainers were ruined.

'This is hopeless,' she said as the rain began.
'Let's try to find some kind of shelter.'
'Look,' Jamie said,
'there's something up ahead.'
He pointed to a little stone hut.
They made their way over to it.
Someone was sitting inside. It was Nick.
'Hi there,' he said. 'Out for a walk?'

'Yes,' Alison said. 'But we got lost.
And we're soaking wet.
I didn't think it would rain today.'
'The weather changes quickly up here,'
Nick said.
'You really need a compass, and proper boots.

'Stay in here till it blows over.
Then I'll take you down to Newchurch.
My car's parked there.
I'll give you a lift back.
Would you like a piece of chocolate?'

While they waited for the rain to stop,
they talked.
Nick told them he helped his Dad out
at the pub in the holidays.
'I'm starting a course at college
in September,' he told them.
'It's at Derby.'
'That's not far from us,' Alison said.
'We live in Nottingham.'

'What made you come to Lancashire?'
Nick asked.
Alison told him about her Mum's hobby.
'She's putting our family tree together,'
she explained.
'That sounds interesting,' Nick said.

'I know quite a bit about mine.
Our family's lived around here
for a long time.
My Uncle Bert once owned your cottage.
He lived there for years.'
'I thought some of the Pendle Witches might
have lived in it,' Jamie said.
Nick laughed. 'I don't think so.
They died in 1612.
That cottage wasn't built until 1850.'

'Do you know much about the witches?'
Alison asked.
'A fair bit,' Nick said. 'But they weren't the kind
of witches you mean.
They didn't have broomsticks and pointy hats.
They were really just sad old women.
Demdike and Old Chattox were rivals.
They each had family to support.
They tried to earn a few pence making spells.

'Don't forget, roads were bad then.
These villages were cut off in winter.
People were superstitious in those days.
They still believed in magic.
Anyone who was a bit odd was called a witch.
If an old woman had a cat or a dog
people thought it was her "familiar".'
'What's a "familiar"?' Jamie asked.
'It was a kind of spirit,' Nick said.
'It did what she told it. Like a servant.'

'We went to Lancaster, yesterday,' Alison said.
'I saw the jail where the witches were tried.'
'Yes, nine of them were sent there,' Nick said.
'Demdike died before the trial began.
It wasn't a very fair trial,' Nick went on.
'No-one spoke up for them.
Little Jennet gave evidence
against her own family.
They hadn't a hope of getting off.
I feel quite sorry for them.'

'The rain's stopped. Shall we go on?
There are things in Newchurch you should see.
Malkin Tower was near there.
That's where the witches used to meet.
They stole a sheep and had a feast there
on Good Friday in 1612.
At the trial it was said
they hatched a plot there –
to blow up Lancaster castle.'

Back at the cottage Alison and Jamie
told their parents all about their day.
'We met Nick on top of Pendle,' Jamie said.
'He took us to see a village where
some of the witches lived.
There's an old grave in the churchyard
with a skull and cross bones on it.
People say that it's a witch's grave.
And there's an eye painted on the church wall.
That was to keep evil spirits away.'

'You've had an exciting time,' Mum said.
'The shop was the best thing,' Jamie went on.
'Don't you think so Alison?
It had life-size witches outside it.
It sells all kinds of things to do with magic.'
Alison smiled. The shop was so normal.
It made the witches seem a harmless tale.
'It's mainly for the tourists,' Jamie said.
'To buy souvenirs to take home.'
Alison had bought a postcard of a black cat.
She would send it to Kelly.

That night Alison was much happier.
The cottage felt more cosy – now she knew
Nick's uncle had lived there.
She liked Nick a lot.
He seemed to like her too.
He had promised to take her and Jamie
out in his car the next day.
She fell asleep looking forward to it.

5

A Souvenir

Alison was woken up by someone
knocking on the door.
She put on her dressing gown
and went downstairs.
Mum was in the kitchen making a cup of tea.
'There's a message for you from Nick,' she said.
'His Dad came over to tell you.
Nick won't be able to take you out today.
He was taken ill in the night.
They've sent for the doctor.'

'What's wrong with him?' Alison asked.
'I'm not sure,' Mum said.
I think he had bad pains in his stomach.'

Alison went cold.
It was starting again. The witchcraft.
She remembered Jamie's words.
'The witches killed the son of the landlord
at the inn. They made clay images of him.'
She thought of the little man
she had found in the café.
The pin of the badge had been pushed
right through its stomach.
She sat down, feeling sick.
'What's the matter?' Mum asked.
'Are you feeling ill too?
Maybe there's a bug going around.'

Alison spent the day alone.
She didn't want to be with the others.
She felt tense and upset. She did not want
anything bad to happen to Nick.

She went into the church.

It was cool and quiet inside.

A woman was putting fresh flowers in vases.

'Did you want to look around dear?' she said.

'I'll come back and lock up later.'

Alison sat down in a pew at the back.

She began to say a prayer.

Others must have come to this church

in the old days, asking for help.

Later, out in the sunlight, she thought

how foolish she had been.

This was the twentieth century.

People didn't believe in magic now.

They didn't die from witches' spells.

Alison had worried over nothing.

On the last day of their holiday Nick called.

'Get your gear together,' he told them.

'If you still want that day out.'

'Nick, you're better!' Alison said.

'I was really worried about you.'

'It was nothing,' Nick said.
'Just one of those 24-hour bugs.
I feel fine now.'

They had a great day out.
Nick showed them a walk through the valley.
Then they climbed up into a wood.
They could see the whole length of Pendle
from there.
'The hill looks like a lion asleep,' Jamie said.
'Squeeze up, you two so I can get a photo
of you both with the hill behind.'
Nick put his arm around Alison.
She felt good, sitting close to him like that.

When they got back Jamie ran on ahead.
Alison was glad to see him go.
She wanted some time alone with Nick.
They stood talking. He took her hand.
Then the egg man came into sight.
At the same time, the black dog ran out
of a garden. Just as he had done before.
It was the same scene all over again.

Alison froze. It had been a perfect day.
She didn't want anything to spoil it.
The dog barked. Nick felt her go tense.
'What's the matter, Alison?' he said
'Sam won't hurt you.
He only wants a bit of fuss.
Old Mrs Jones, his owner, is getting on.
She can't take him for long walks.
That's why he barks at everyone.
He's asking you to take him out.
Come on then, boy, good dog.'

Alison pointed to the egg man.
'Who's that?' she asked.
'That's old Charlie,' Nick said.
'He's a bit of a joke around here.
He's as blind as a bat. And so clumsy.
He's always falling down and breaking
his eggs. I don't know how he makes a living.'
'He was very rude to me,' Alison said.
'He would be,' Nick said. 'The old devil
enjoys upsetting people.
But he doesn't mean any harm.'

Alison began to relax.
There was a simple explanation for all
the things that had happened.
She had been so stupid to let
Jamie's talk of witches get to her.
She stood close to Nick.
'Give me your phone number,' he said.
'I'll ring you when you get home.
When I come to Derby we can meet.
This is not goodbye.
I'll be over to see you off in the morning.'

The cottage was tidy.
The car was packed.
Dad checked the oil and petrol.
'Time we were off,' he told Alison.
'We can't wait any longer.
We've a long journey ahead.'
'Just a few more minutes,' Alison begged.
'I know Nick will come to say goodbye.'

Just then his car came into view.
Nick jumped out.
'Sorry I'm late,' he said.
'I went to buy you these souvenirs.'
Jamie ripped the paper off his.
Inside was a compass.
'Thanks,' Jamie said. 'Just what I needed.'

Alison's present was a tiny witch riding
on a broomstick.
It had a loop at the back.
'Thanks a lot,' she said. 'I'll hang it up
in my bedroom.
I'll never forget the witches of Pendle!'